TV-Station Secrets

By Dave Cupp and Cecilia Minden

The
Child's
World®
www.childsworld.com

Published in the United States of America by The Child's World®
1980 Lookout Drive • Mankato, MN 56003-1705
800-599-READ • www.childsworld.com

ACKNOWLEDGMENTS

The Child's World® : Mary Berendes, Publishing Director

Produced by Shoreline Publishing Group LLC
President / Editorial Director: James Buckley, Jr.
Designer: Tom Carling, carlingdesign.com
Cover Art: Slimfilms
Assistant Editor: Jim Gigliotti

Photo Credits:
Cover: iStock (main); Courtesy Cecilia Minden, Photos.com
(insets)
Interior: AP/Wide World: 20, 23, 26; Corbis: 16; Getty Images: 6, 7,
17, 22, 28, 29; Courtesy Cecilia Minden: 8, 13, 14; Dreamstime.com
(photographers listed): Gary Blakeley 9, Soundsweeps 18; iStock: 4,
11, 24

LIBRARY OF CONGRESS CATALOG-IN-PUBLICATION DATA

Cupp, Dave.
 TV-station secrets / by Dave Cupp, Cecilia Minden.
  p. cm. — (Reading rocks!)
 Includes bibliographical references and index.
 ISBN 978-1-60253-104-8 (library bound : alk. paper)
 1. Television broadcasting of news—Juvenile literature. I.
Minden, Cecilia. II. Title. III. Series.

 PN4784.T4C87 2008
 070.1'95—dc22

                        2008004487

CONTENTS

WHEN NEWS Breaks

There's a fire downtown! A truck full of oranges has overturned on the highway! A major snowstorm has caused all the schools to close! Quick . . . send out the TV news crew!

Every local television station has several newscasts each day. They tell big stories and small ones, along with weather and sports. On the screen, you see news **anchors**, **meteorologists**, and sportscasters. What you don't see are all the people behind the scenes.

In this book, we'll find out who these people are, how they do their jobs, and the steps it takes to bring the news to you!

OPPOSITE PAGE
Many hours of work by a team of people ends with the evening-news TV show.

Anchors are the main people who read the news during a broadcast.

How does a story get on TV? The first step is making **assignments**. In the morning, the staff talks over which stories to cover.

News stories come from many **sources**. Reporters search the Internet, newspapers, and magazines. They talk to people and officials all over town. Some ideas come from national sources such as the Associated Press.

On the Beat

A reporter is frequently assigned to a **beat**. This means he or she focuses on one type of news. A beat could be City Hall, the school board, police, or another part of the community. The reporter checks with sources every day, attends meetings, and gets to know the hot topics.

After the meeting, the assignment **editor** chooses which stories go to each reporter. Do you ever get assignments you don't really want to do? So do reporters! Not every story can be a big one. But it takes many stories to put together a newscast. The editor keeps track of the stories during the day.

Producers and editors meet often to decide which stories they will report.

The video-grapher chooses the best place for the reporter to stand to get the best shot.

With the assignment in hand, the reporter has to go "on location." This means the reporter goes to where the news is being made. The reporter doesn't go alone. He or she needs a **videographer**. It's hard to have a TV news story without pictures to go with it!

The videographer drives the "live truck" to the scene of the news. This truck is filled with gear that can send video back to the TV station— and into thousands of homes instantly.

The large disk on top of this truck is a **satellite** dish. It's used to send pictures from the news scene to the TV station.

When the videographer gets to the scene, he has to make quick choices. Viewers will "see" the events through his eye. So he needs to know which pictures to take to tell the story. Whenever you see a reporter battling a storm or at the site of a big fire, remember that a videographer is behind the camera bringing the pictures home to you.

One good way for a reporter to find out information is to do an **interview**. This means asking people questions to learn what's going on.

For some interviews, the people being interviewed are friendly and want to help. But other times, a reporter has to ask people questions they might not want to answer!

Reporters learn to ask good questions and to help people be comfortable telling their stories. Sometimes reporters need to be charming, but other times they need to be tough. Are you good at talking to people? Imagine that you have a chance to interview your favorite actor or sports hero. You would want him or her to like and respect you. If you're a good reporter, you can do both.

A reporter also needs to care about people and to be a good storyteller.

She tells TV viewers the stories of people affected by the news. The videographer shows us who and what the reporter is talking about. A reporter needs to understand complicated things but explain them simply—and quickly. The average news story is only about 45 to 90 seconds long!

While the videographer takes the pictures of the subject, the reporter (far left) asks questions.

GETTING NEWS on the Air

After the reporter and the videographer go back to the station, the producer goes to work. It's her job to put the video and the story together for the broadcast. Brynne Tuggle is a producer for the morning news show at a North Carolina station.

"I come to work when most people are going to bed. I arrive around 11:30 P.M. and gather stories for the two one-hour morning shows. It's my job to fill those two shows with news of interest to our audience."

First, Brynne reviews the stories from the night before. She begins to think about which anchor will read them. "Each anchor has their own style of speaking. I try to match the stories to the anchors."

Brynne has to juggle many different stories at one time.

"The hardest part about being a producer is telling the story in the shortest amount of time. We sometimes have just a few seconds!"

Now it's time to "stack" the show. This means Brynne decides the order in which the stories will appear on TV. Brynne uses a computer program to help her. The program has slots for everything that should be in the newscast. Brynne puts each anchor's initials by the stories they will read on the air.

Each newscast is divided into segments of time called **blocks**. The first segment is also called the A-Block. It opens with the **lead**.

This chart shows how one part of a broadcast will be organized.

W	FIRST WEATHER	WEATHER WALL	WXWALL		1:05	0:00	1
LL	WEATHER OUT	THREE SHOT	3SHOT		0:15	0:00	0
					0:00	0:00	0
G	RDU TRAVEL	OTS: RDU	OTS		0:17	0:00	0
g	toss to anthony	TAKE LIVE EFX	LIVE EFX		0:00	0:00	0
W	L-RDU TRAVEL	TAKE ANTHONY LIVE	LIVE		0:15	0:00	0
W	P-RDU TRAVEL	TAKE VTR	PKG	NO	0:00	0:45	0
W	T-RDU TRAVEL	TAKE ANTHONY LIVE	LIVE		0:15	0:00	0
					0:00	0:00	0
C	TRAVEL ON THE ROA	OTS: Holiday Travel	OTS		0:10	0:00	0
	toss to sheyenne	TAKE LIVE EFX	LIVE EFX		0:00	0:00	0
RO	L-TRAVEL ON THE RO	TAKE SHEYENNE LIV	LIVE		0:15	0:00	0
RO	P-TRAVEL ON THE RO	TAKE VTR	PKG	YES	0:00	0:45	0
SRO	T-TRAVEL ON THE RO	TAKE SHEYENNE LIV	LIVE		0:15	0:00	0
					0:00	0:00	0

Timing

Each broadcast must be timed exactly. Each anchor enters his or her rate of speaking into a news computer. The computer then counts exactly how long it will take for each anchor to read the story during the newscast.

"The lead is important because you want to catch the viewers' attention," says Brynne. The A-Block is followed by a commercial, which is followed by the B-Block. Other blocks will contain more news and sports.

Most newscasts start with blocks of hard news, which are important stories of recent events. Brynne's morning show also includes local traffic news.

Instead of filming a story ahead of time, some reports go on the air live.

During a newscast, stories come in all lengths. People in the news business use these cool words to describe different types of stories.

Reader: When an anchor tells a short story without video.

Voiceover (VO): When an anchor reads the story while video is shown to the viewers.

Sound bite: A short piece that shows the person being interviewed on camera. It's also known as "sound on tape."

Package: A longer story with several pieces of video, usually including a live or recorded shot of a reporter speaking to the viewers.

Live shots: When the viewer watches a reporter telling the story as it happens.

Talkers: Also called "bumps," these are mini-stories that connect larger stories, or when two anchors chat with one another.

Kicker: The last story on a newscast, it's usually something touching or fun—like video of a water-skiing squirrel!

The anchor reads her words when the camera operator says to start.

Sharing the News

Local stations often share their news with stations in other cities. Many stations belong to national **networks** such as NBC, CBS, and ABC. The network stations share their work among each other. That way, viewers can see news from around the country or even around the world.

Brynne is almost ready for today's broadcast. She has "stacked" her newscast with all the types of stories she needs.

Brynne might also work on video in the **edit bay**. The edit bay has equipment that can stitch together pictures and stories to make the parts of the newscast work the best. Reporters and videographers also use the edit bay to find the best shots that match their stories.

Then it's time to go on the air. The camera crews in the studio are ready. The anchors are in their chairs. The **director** counts down. "And now, the morning news."

An edit bay is filled with video gear that helps editors and producers create stories for the news.

THE NEWS
Team

Newscasts aren't just stories covered by news reporters. Most TV news shows also make room for weather and sports.

A meteorologist, or weather reporter, is a scientist who understands how weather works. He can predict what the weather will be like in the near future. Most people watching newscasts are very interested in the weather. They want to know what clothes to wear or if they need to take an umbrella to work.

Meteorologists study information from satellites and **radar** to understand what's happening in their area. They might also check thermometers or other gauges. Weather isn't always predictable, but good meteorologists will be able to give accurate **forecasts** most of the time.

Meteorologists study computers, maps, and other things to find out what they need to know.

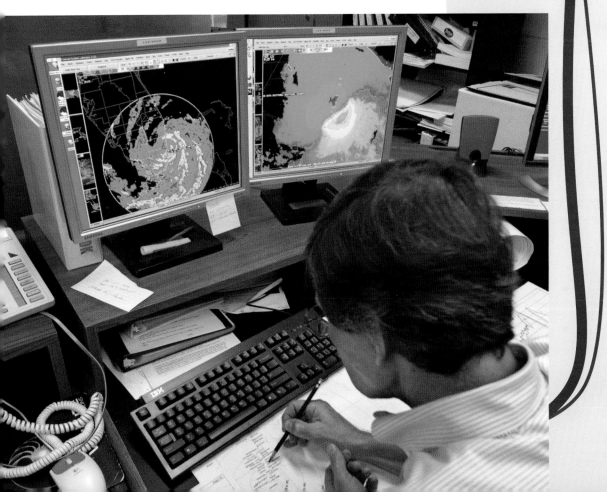

SAT   SUN

79°

Am I Blue?

During the newscast, the meteorologist stands in front of a blank wall usually painted green or blue. This is called the chroma-key (KROH-muh KEE) wall. The weather maps you see on TV are not really on the wall behind the meteorologist. They are projected electronically. The reporter actually sneaks peeks at the maps on a TV that you can't see.

Meteorologists need the same skills as reporters. They have to make a lot of information easy to understand in a short amount of

During big weather events, reporters sometimes go into the storm to describe what they see.

Meteorologists sometimes show viewers photos that were taken by satellites spinning high above Earth.

time. The meteorologist is the only member of the news team who tells us what will happen tomorrow instead of reporting what happened yesterday or today.

People make important decisions based on a meteorologist's forecast. For example, a dangerous storm might be heading for a major city. The meteorologist lets people know if they need to move to a safer location.

Sports reporters have to be right where the action is.

Some people think sports reporters have the best job at the TV station. Not only do they get to go to all sorts of sport events, they get paid to watch them!

The sportscaster faces many of the same challenges as a news reporter. He needs to capture the story of each contest. In just a few seconds and with carefully chosen pictures, he shows the highlights of games.

A sportscaster also needs to be good at doing interviews. He needs to prepare his questions so he can get the information he needs.

A sportscaster should enjoy all sports. He might have a favorite sport such as football, basketball, or baseball. But viewers love many sorts of sports, so he needs to include them all in his reports. Some sportscasters are actually former athletes.

Sportscasters on the news are different than sports announcers. Those people describe the action of a sport while it is happening, not after it is over.

In smaller towns, the sportscaster might also be the videographer— he or she films games to describe later on the air.

On most Friday or Saturday nights, there are sports events all over. Sportscasters must decide which events are the most important ones to cover. The station sends videographers to as many games as possible. The cameras record every play, but only the most important ones will be seen on the air.

Sportscasters go into locker rooms after the games to interview coaches and players. The sportscaster asks questions to get information and opinions about what happened in the game.

A sportscaster only has about five minutes to tell viewers about sports from all over. He must also cover

Reporters crowd around an athlete after a big game to get the story for TV viewers.

any breaking sports stories (such as a big trade or an important race result). Sportscasters have to choose which stories and sports to include in each broadcast. They must also check their work carefully to make sure that they have all the scores exactly right. It's a fun job, but it's a lot of work!

During a news show, the director uses a panel of buttons and switches like this one to send the show out to viewers.

As the newscast begins, other people go to work behind the scenes. For the next hour, Brynne will watch and listen to the newscast. She is ready to make a change if news breaks during the show. She might have to rearrange her whole stack in just a few minutes! But most days, her hardest work is done when the show begins.

During the broadcast, the anchors speak while looking at the camera. They're reading from a machine called a **teleprompter**. The anchors look into the camera but read the words going across the teleprompter's screen. Anchors also have a tiny speaker in one ear. The producer or director can talk to the anchor without viewers hearing what they're saying.

After the anchor reads the kicker, the news team "signs off." The newscast is over . . . now it's time to get ready for the next show. The news never stops happening!

The viewers only see a few people on TV, but it takes many others to get the show on the air.

GLOSSARY

anchors the main people who read the news during a TV broadcast

assignments stories reporters are sent to cover

beat the type of news a certain reporter usually covers

blocks sections of time during a newscast

director the person in charge of a TV broadcast

edit bay the place where editing is done

editor at a newspaper or TV station, an editor is a person who is in charge; the assignment editor is in charge of handing out assignments

forecasts predictions, in this case, of the weather

interview to ask someone questions

lead the first story during a newscast

meterologists scientists who study the weather

networks large groups of TV stations

producers the people on a TV crew who organize the team's work

radar a machine that shows what is in the air, such as clouds or airplanes

satellite a communication machine that orbits Earth

sources people or places that provide information to a reporter

teleprompter a machine that shows a TV anchor what words to say on the air

FIND OUT MORE

BOOKS

How Do I Become a TV Reporter?
by Mindy Englart
(Blackbirch Press, 2003)
Find out how you can learn the skills to interview people,
work with cameras, and be part of a news team.

Lights, Camera, Action!
by Lisa O'Brien
(Maple Tree Press, 2001)
This book includes information on how TV shows are made, as
well as how movies are put together.

Working at a TV Station
by Gary Davis
(Children's Press, 1999)
Learn even more about the many jobs at a TV station.

WEB SITES

Visit our Web site for lots of links about TV news, reporters, and
TV stations: www.childsworld.com/links

Note to Parents, Teachers, and Librarians: We routinely check our Web links to
make sure they're safe, active sites—so encourage your readers to check them out!

INDEX

DAVE CUPP is a professor at the University of North Carolina, where he works with student journalists. He was formerly the news director of a TV station in Virginia.

CECILIA MINDEN is a writer, editor, and reading expert who has written many books for young readers.